THE WORLD OF
TWILIGHT
MONK
VOLUME 1

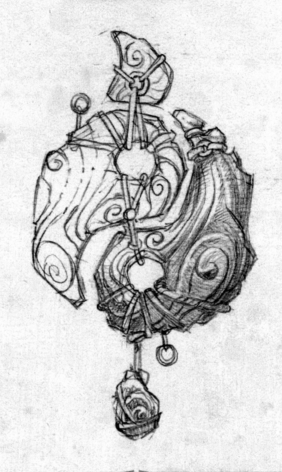

WRITTEN AND ILLUSTRATED BY:
TRENT KANIUGA

Additional Art BY:
Danny Kong
Marcus Luk
Domen Kozelj

CONTENTS

CHARACTERS
THE WORLD OF TWILIGHT MONK

RAZIEL TENZA
EXILED MONK

Raziel Tenza has become the living vessel for the Monks of Twilight - Ancient, celestial, spirits of the greatest warrior monks of all time. At times, they pull him into the Shadow Realm and teach him legendary, forgotten Kung Fulio techniques. Upon returning to the physical realm, he is fated to roam the lands of Speria in search of Darksprites in order to seal the many world gates and prevent the coming of 5th age.

Raz is hot-headed, reckless, daring, and awkward, with a style of kung fulio that is fierce and unpredictable.

AGE: 15
RACE: Moonken
WEAPON: Fist, Bo Staff, Blessed Carrot, Phantom Pillar

RAZIEL TENZA
MODEL SHEET

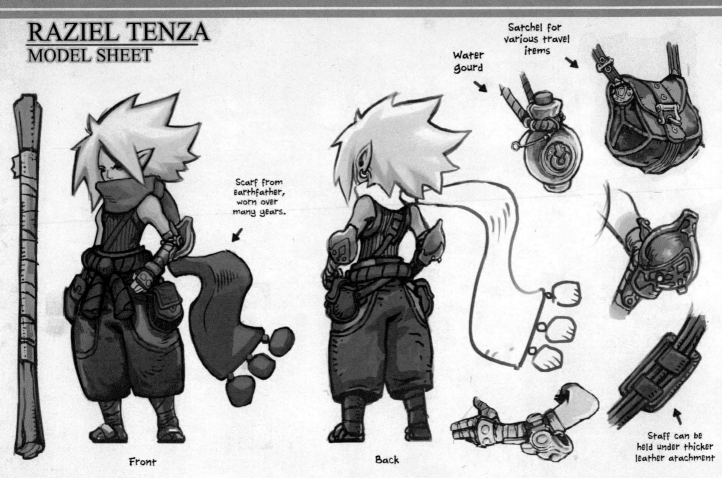

Scarf from earthfather, worn over many years.

Water gourd

Satchel for various travel items

Staff can be held under thicker leather atachment

Front

Back

Undies

Crescent Isle monk robes.

Various weapons and adventure items

Crescent Isle emblem

Symbol of a sealed magic

TWILIGHT MONKS
ANCIENT SEALED MASTERS
CHARACTER SHEET

Bound For Eternity

Long ago, the Monks of the Twilight were fierce warrior monks whose sole purpose was to maintain the balance between chaos and order in Speria.

Failing to sustain that balance, over time, the world had been consumed in a Storm of Shadows. In order to preserve the world of the living, the Monks of Twilight had to make the ultimate sacrifice. They'd sealed themselves, along with all of the Darksprites within the pillar. In doing so, they themselves had been bound for eternity.

When Raz shatters the pillar, his body transforms into the vessel of the Monks of Twilight.

Body is completely made of smoke

Raziel Is The Vessel

At times, the Monks of Twilight will pull Raz's consciousness into the Shadow Realm, a mystical dojo beyon space and time. There, they train the young Moonken in their lost art of sealing Darksprites. But Raz can only enter the Dojo of the Shadow Realm once he has mastered his own emotions. If he cannot, their secrets may be lost forever, and the world will become over-run with dark shadows once more.

NORA ANAKO
THE SHORT FUSE

Nora strives for disciplined perfection, and refuses to let anyone or anything keep her from shining in the eyes of Master Dou and the other elders at the Monastery.

A master of the boomerang and strategic battle, Nora is one of the few monks to study under the great master Jyazo, and survive without critical injury. She will take on the tasks that most monk trainees fear and come out unscathed.

Because of her tactical nature, she is slow to act, but once she does, her approach is calculated and deadly, but always by-the-book.

AGE: 15
RACE: Moonken
WEAPON: Boomerang

NORA ANAKO
MODEL SHEET

RIBBONS TIE PIGTAILS TOGETHER.

BOOMERANG PRIMARY WEAPON OF CHOICE (ATTACHES TO BACK)

LEATHER WRAPPING UNDER ROPE TIE.

METAL GAUNTLETS CONNECT ELBOW SHIELDS.

front

Back

Undies

Alt mission gear

CRESCENT ISLE EMBLEM

CRESCENT ISLE MONK ROBES.

RIN TORRA
THE MIGHTY SMALL FRY

All of his life, Rin had constantly studied the "Ninja Arts Weekly" newsletters from cover to cover, dreaming of one day becoming a stealth master of Ninjitsu like his idol, the author of the pamphlet newsletter, Master Kito. This practice was somewhat discouraged, due to the fact that many of the principals of Ninjitsu deviated from the style of martial arts that was taught at the monastery at Crescent Isle.

This only meant that Rin had to become even MORE secretive about his fascination with throwing stars, smoke pellets, and climbing spikes, which likely derives from his fear of confrontation.

Rin is the peacekeeper of the trio of orphans, usually by way of providing food to calm conflicts. Rin has a big heart, and an even bigger stomach, will always follow orders, and is incredibly loyal.

AGE: 15
RACE: Moonken
WEAPON: Kunai, Ninja Stars, Ghost Poo, nunchuck

RIN TORRA
MODEL SHEET

Banana

Satchel

Ham Sandwich

NINJA ARTS WEEKLY

Ninja Arts Magazine

Fist Guard

Smoke Pellets

Climbing Claws

Throwing Stars

Front

Back

Undies

Robes

Alt Travel Gear

DEZMIN DUKRAL
ROGUE SWORDSMAN

Formerly of the imperial blademasters of Liongate, Dezmin is a hunted wanderer. He is always calm and collected, so long as he has his flask of whiskey. The more alcohol he has had, the better swordsman he becomes. He will always assure you that he has a plan... even if it's the wrong one. "It's better to travel a hundred miles in the wrong direction, than to not move anywhere at all".

Betrayed by his commanding officer and branded a traitor, to be relentlessly tracked by bounty hunters. Now he wanders from town to town,

dreaming only of peace and quiet, a guitar and a little potato farm somewhere where no one will ever find him.

In every town which Dezmin visits, more hungry bounty hunters line up to kill him, thus adding another name to his already large list of victims.

AGE: 27
RACE: Human
WEAPON: Sword, Guitar or Whiskey

DEZMIN DUKRAL
MODEL SHEET

SYMBOL OF A CRANE.

A DEMON IS CAPTURED WITHIN THIS TRINKET.

LIONGATE REJECTION PLATE. SENT TO CANDIDATES WHO DIDN'T MAKE THE CUT.

NECKLACE SYMBOL REPRESENTS A PART OF DEZMIN'S PAST.

GUITAR FROM LONG GONE ERA DEZMIN CARRIES IT WITH HIM AS HE IS TRYING TO "GIVE UP THE SWORD"..

Front

Back

DEZMIN'S BLADE MASTER OF LIONGATE UNIFORM.

MASTER DOU
EVERLASTING KNOW-IT-ALL
CHARACTER SHEET

Conceals strength

KEY DATA

AGE - 149
RACE - Moonken
WEAPONS - Mind

Echoes of Twilight

The Monks who remain within the Celestial Temple on Crescent Isle are but a mere echo of the ancient and forgotten ways of the Monks of Twilight. As the leader of the Council of Elders, it is up to Master Dou to interpret the forgotten texts to guide new Moonken as they enter into training at the Monastery. The Moonken do not choose sides, they only maintain the balance of disputes. Master Dou and the high council are steadfast in this fundamental ideology. Others believe in a more altruistic translation. This difference is the primary reason many have aligned with the Celestial Temple, and why others choose to leave.

MASTER YOBEI
A MONK ON THE EDGE
CHARACTER SHEET

Paseo Paswagi

KEY DATA

AGE - 56
RACE - Moonkcn
WEAPONS - Peo Paswagi

Traveler Teacher

Yobei is a teacher at the Monastery at Crescent Isle. Although he is carries the title of "Master", he is not part of the Circle of Elders, and he struggles with his faith. At times he will disappear on spiritual walk-abouts for months on end. His former master had betrayed the monastery, which left him constantly questioning their ways. It is because of this that he is assigned to teach the worst performing students at the monastery, namely Raz, Nora and Rin. Yobei is seldom very hands on as a teacher, but tends to show up at the last second to bail them out of their own mess.

MASTER VEE
MEDICINE MASTER
CHARACTER SHEET

Scroll Pouch

Medicine Pouch

Purification Beads

KEY DATA

AGE - 165
RACE - Moonken
WEAPONS - Medicine Case

A Dream of Peace

Master Vee swore off violence decades ago. He believes in healing the world through deep meditation, and surfing. After losing his memory for the first 120 years of his life, he smokes halucination inducing substances to unlock his memory. He believes that he had discovered some secret about the Monastery and Crescent isle. But the truth of it eludes him. Therefore he spends all of his time in solitude, and digging through old texts.

TOMO
CELESTIAL CHAMBERLAIN
CHARACTER SHEET

Monastery Keyring

KEY DATA

AGE - ???
RACE - ???
WEAPONS - None

Mysterious Keymaster

No one really knows where Tomo comes from. But his devotion to Master Dou has earned the trust of the entire council of elders. No one gains passage into the Monastery, or it's many locked doors without first getting past Tomo. He is unwavering in his devotion to Master Dou, and loyal till his dying breath.

MASTER KLU
THE GROOVY MASTER
CHARACTER SHEET

KEY DATA

AGE - 64
RACE - Moonken
WEAPONS - None

Relic Collector

Master Klu spends his time restoring the old dojo on the abandoned north end of the island when he's not teaching classes.

From his relaxed demeanor and sleeping habits, one would not suspect that he knows anything about self discipline or fighting at all, but rumors abound of his once more adventurous years, leaving everyone to wonder if there's much more to the old hermit that would rather be surfing than teaching.

MASTER KOZOMO
THE SPIRIT MASTER
CHARACTER SHEET

KEY DATA

AGE - 84
RACE - Moonken
WEAPONS - None

Eternal Custodian

Master Kozomo no longer posesses a body in our dimension. He claims that he'd lost his physical form long ago, and continues to phase shift between realities. In our world, he seems to live as a pure form of energy, but he insists that his true physical form exists in some distant universe beyond time and space which no one else can percieve.

This claim appears to be true, as he hasn't appeared to age in over 300 years. Since he does not posess a body, his interactions with this realm are very limited and acts primarily as a custodian for the ancient libraries of the monastery.

MASTER TOKKA
THE LOST SAGE
CHARACTER SHEET

KEY DATA

AGE - 159
RACE - Moonken
WEAPONS - Staff Of
Three Kings

Staff of Three Kings

Red

Echoes of Twilight

When word of a revolt in Arcturo reached the Celestial Temple, The Elders immediately dispatched Tokka to the restore peace to the region. On his own, he was powerless to stop them, but using the Staff of Three Kings, he was able to seal the rogue Magma Unit within mountain along with himself. For fifty years he's had to live with his failure. Now the three brothers threaten to open the Dragon gate if the barrier is not lifted, and Tokka's mind is not as focused as it once was. The extreme isolation over the years has left him rather excitable, spastic, and incoherant, a mere shadow of the once powerful Master of Kung Fulio.

MASTER YIBADA
THE UNNATURALLY GIFTED
CHARACTER SHEET

KEY DATA

AGE - 32
RACE - Gu
WEAPONS - Elemental
Gauntlets

Friend or Foe

Master Yibada is the only Non-Moonkin resident of the Monastery to recieve the title of "Master". Several years ago, he arrived on the Celestial Temple doorstep and sat for 30 days without food or water. When asked to leave by the Council of Elders, he fought and defeated all but Master Dou.

Originally from the Lizard-Men known only as The Gu, Yibada became so obsessed with martial arts that he found no challengers worthy of battle, until he sparred with Master Dou. It is unheard of for anyone other than a Moonken to achieve the rank of Master, but after his incredible display of power, they had no choice but to accept him as one of their own or face him as an enemy.

ORCHID
THE IMMORTAL DECEIVER
CHARACTER SHEET

KEY DATA

AGE - 1015
RACE - ???
WEAPONS - Various
Forbidden Magics

Horns grow longer with each passing year

Mask conceals true face

Symbol of the Stormshadows and Orchids ever watching eye

Trinkets all infused with magic abilities

Trinkets woven throughout hair

Eternal Twilight

A mysterious witch that dwells within the world tree. Orchid is the last remaining of her kind, and is over one thousand years old. Her kind were sealed away, and forgotten as legend over a thousand years ago. Through various rituals, she has discovered a kind of twisted immortality. The cost of her youthful beauty is that she must steal the remaining years of life away from others.

If she fails to feed her lifeblood, she will wither, tormented within her empty bones eternally.

She sends her minions, the Storm Shadows to scour the land in search of the pillar, and other forbidden magics.

This year marks her "Sweet 1016th" Birthday.

STORM SHADOWS
MINIONS OF THE WORLD TREE
CHARACTER SHEET

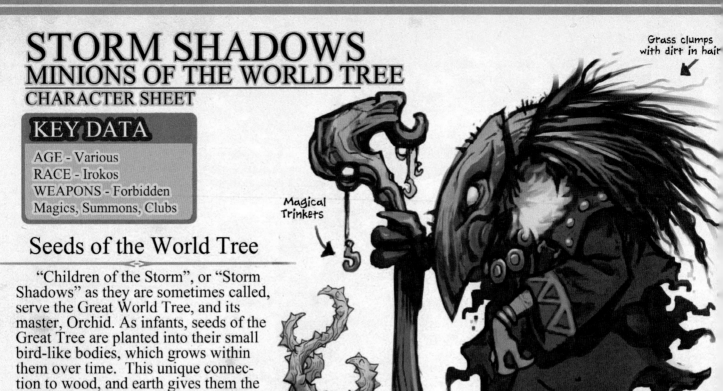

KEY DATA

AGE - Various
RACE - Irokos
WEAPONS - Forbidden
Magics, Summons, Clubs

Grass clumps
with dirt in hair

Magical
Trinkets

Seeds of the World Tree

"Children of the Storm", or "Storm Shadows" as they are sometimes called, serve the Great World Tree, and its master, Orchid. As infants, seeds of the Great Tree are planted into their small bird-like bodies, which grows within them over time. This unique connection to wood, and earth gives them the ability to manipulate trees and roots. However, the relationship is more of a command, enslaving the wood to the will of the World Tree.

Strangling
Thorns

Twig
Legs

IROKOMANCERS
WOOD SUMMONERS
CHARACTER SHEET

Seedlings

Bone
Masks

Treeling

Iroko Minions

Storm Shadows are named so, for their purpose. Created by Orchid to seek out any artifacts with magical properties, they aim to find and release the "Darksprites" which will bring about the coming storm, and plunge the world into a new age, where they believe they will be reborn as humans, and inherit the world.
Iroko Minions are lesser forms and act only as an extension of the mind of their creator. Their incessant verbal abuse and vulgar taunts make them particularly agitating.

STORMSHADOWS
ARMY OF BIRDMEN
CHARACTER SHEET

Elite Storm Shadow

Most Common Form

Bone Masks give them a sense of individualism.

Birdbrains

Stormshadows believe that they will be reborn as humans, and inherit the world in the 5th age, so long as they faithfully serve the will of Orchid. Because they hold no self value in their current form, they will stop at nothing to accomplish her goal, even sacrificing their own lives to acquire forbidden magics for her.

Because they are given consciousness from the seeds of the world tree, they share a kinship with all plant-life, and may commune with the elements. However they spend most of their cognitive thoughts drowning out the soothing voices of the world around them in favor of repeating the hateful mantras of their religion

AZUMAT
FROSTBITE DEMON
CHARACTER SHEET

KEY DATA

AGE - 2000+
RACE - Darksprite
WEAPONS -
Bone Arms, Frost Breath

A Frostbite Fury

Resurrected and summoned into the world as a failed attempt to subdue the three Brothers of the Bali Kajaa in the Arcturo Mountains, Azumat's sole desire is to cover the world in ice for his frozen army. After thousands of years trapped in a state of suspended animation, his anger has only consumed him further.

Back

RODIN
DEFILED HAMMER KNIGHT
CHARACTER SHEET

KEY DATA

AGE - 46
RACE - Human
WEAPONS - Hammer of The Shattered Sun

Hammer of the Shattered Sun

Back

Knight in the Nightmare

Last remaining member of the Knights of Locke, and doomed to wander the hollow caverns and cold mountainside of Arcturo, Rodin is haunted by the ghosts of his former unit. He believes that he died along with his brethren, and that the mountain is a form of purgatory. Stirring in his lonesome madness, He awaits the arrival of a great warrior to carry him to the infinite. Only through battle may his soul be released.

DOKEN
TOAD WARRIOR DARKSPRITE
CHARACTER SHEET

KEY DATA

AGE - ???
RACE - Darksprite
WEAPONS -
Spear, Tongue

Anchient Toad Warrior

Doken is a Darksprite that has spent almost 100 years encased in stone, among Master Klu's secret stash collection of artifacts and weapons.

Sealed form

UMU
FORTUNE TELLER
CHARACTER SHEET

KEY DATA

AGE - ???
RACE - Dragon
WEAPONS - Ultimate knowledge of the universe

Fortune or Fiction?

Umu is one of the oldest living dragons in the world of Speria. He sees many timelines all at once, giving him the ability to tell you the outcome of any of your actions. Such information would be considered very useful, if one could tolerate his arrogant, condescending tone. Umu's abilities are matched only by his boastful self importance. Because of this, he presently resides in a small urn burried in Master Klu's secret stash.

BYRON
MAYOR OF GIANT'S CROWN
CHARACTER SHEET

KEY DATA

AGE - 58
RACE - Human
WEAPONS -
Public Relations

Back

Gold
and
Diamond
Cane

On The Back of a Giant

Mayor of Giant's Crown and liaison for those living in the peaches above the great city. Byron is a calculating opportunist, ever seeking an advantage to exploit, in order to line his pockets. Born in the export city of Belgarde, as a child Byron learned to pickpocket to survive the rough streets of the bustling city. After getting caught red handed, he fled to Giant's Crown. There, he accrued tremendous debt in the pursuit of the many "opportunities" and "get rich quick" schemes presented on every corner. This of course, led to a horrible gambling addiction, until he was recruited by D. Dorville eventually becoming his right hand man, delivering "peach pins" to those who Dorville deemed worthy. It wasn't until the people had turned on Dorville, and locked him away in the crack, that Byron took on the office of Mayor, and vowed to never lose the favor of the common people. Until, of course, he could himself ascend to become a peacher.

DINDLE
PINT-SIZED BUTLER
CHARACTER SHEET

KEY DATA

AGE - 29
RACE - Dwarf
WEAPONS - 3 Piece Suit,
Spare Change, Soap Box

Tattered
Hat
Dindle

DINDLE

Crate
adds 12
inches.

Crate

A Loyal Servant

Dindle has served as Byron's right hand man since he was a child. Once merely a beggar at the TOE of the giant, Byron took him in and gave him a job. Not much is known about dindle, other than that he has developed a taste for finer things, and looks down on those less fortunate with disdain. Due to his short stature, he carries a crate for extra height when he needs to have greater prescense or stand tall next to other men.

NOX
THE RIVAL
CHARACTER SHEET

KEY DATA

AGE - 16
RACE - Moonken
WEAPONS - Bo Staff,
Big Mouth, Bad Attitude

Red Cobras
#&*%'ng
RULE!

← Power
Pomp

← Bo
Staff

Respect Through Power

Once the apprentice of Master Yibada,
until he felt that he'd outgrown his
teachings. Soon after, Nox splintered off
and started his own unit, "The Red
Cobras". Nox is stubborn, boastfull, and
power hungry. He trains constantly, and
is well known to be the best martial arts
student in Crescent Isle under the
Masters. "If you're not the best, then you
SUCK!" is his motto. He believes in
survival of the fittest, and maintains his
army of followers through propaganda
newsletters and staged fights. He loves
to make bets, and has never lost.

RED COBRAS
NOX'S CRONIES
CHARACTER SHEET

KEY DATA

AGE - 14-17
RACE - Moonken
WEAPONS - Various,

Red Cobras
Emblem

Bolo

Diego

A Band of Misfits

The Red Cobras began to follow
Nox after a rumor that he'd once
beaten Master Yibada in combat.
This rumor was never contested by
the Lizard Master since he left the
Monastery soon after.

Many of Nox's followers believe
that strength is all that matters in the
world of Kung Fulio, a philosophy
which he endlessly preaches. Nox
offers these followers a "Cheat Sheet
to Kung Fulio" through a members
only weekly newsletter for 10 pinny.

GRAY
THE RAVEN BLADE
CHARACTER SHEET

KEY DATA

AGE - 26
RACE - Partial Human + ?
WEAPONS - Infused
Metal Blades

A Demon From The Past

Once a member of the elite swordsman known as The Fangs of Liongate, Gray studied directly under Dezmin Dukral. Once his master was convicted of crimes against the throne, Gray went on a hellbent journey for revenge, to hunt down the traitor and bring him to justice. In the lowest realms of the Earthshells, known as "The Bottom of the World", he forged a pact with a Darksprite, imbuing him with the power of the Living Blade. The symbiotic relationship has warped his mind, and turned him into a killing machine.

SAMORA
THE BANDIT SWORDSMAN
CHARACTER SHEET

KEY DATA

AGE - 29
RACE - Human
WEAPONS - Various
Enchanted Blades

A Bandit Swordsman

Samora leads a band of rogues and theives, looting supply caravans and robbing any less than cautious travelers. He is known as the Bandit Swordsman due to his affinity for bladed weapons. He is not particularly skilled with them, but each sword posesses a unique ability. For instance, one cut from the Blade of Sorrow, is said leave men weaping uncontrollably, dehydrating its victim until death. The Crooked blade shatters the spine, the Earthblade, will turn a man to stone and so forth.

MAGMA UNIT
THE THREE WISHES
CHARACTER SHEET

Twisted by Fate

Chutar

Kartooj

Denoza

The Bali Kajaa

Many years ago, three brothers of the Bali Kajaa discovered the Staff of Three Kings deep in the heart of the mountain. When they touched the staff, a Fury awoke, and offered to grant them each a wish. Being a warrior race, they each sought mastery over their fighting abilities to bring honor to their kind. But their wishes transformed them into power hungry beasts. Now twisted and obsessed with domination, the three brothers demanded that the Bali Kajaa elders finally reveal their strength to the world, and open the Dragon Gate. But they refused, and in the conflict, the entire mountain was sealed, and their once great city city was destroyed.

CHUTAR
THE FIRESTORM
CHARACTER SHEET

KEY DATA

AGE - 37
RACE - Bali Kajaa
WEAPONS - Fire Breath, Flaming Glass Shards

Breath Of The Mountain

As the eldest brother, and leader of the Magma Unit, Chutar had always been ambitious. But his transformation pushed him over the edge. Now imbued with a glass body, impervious to the fire of the Mountain, Chutar ravaged the Sky Temple and torched the forests surrounding Arcturo. He has no remorse, and seeks revenge upon the human world for sealing him and his brothers away in the mountain valley, amongst the rubble of their once great civilization.

KARTOOJ
THE ARROW
CHARACTER SHEET

Scaled Gold Plates

Bladed Gauntlet Cuts When Dashing

Leather Wraps

KEY DATA

AGE - 35
RACE - Bali Kajaa
WEAPONS - Bladed
Gauntlet, Fierce Speed

The Fast And The Furious

Kartooj was also once a student of the Bali Kajaa, and a defender of the Dragon Gate in the mountains of Arcturo. The power of the Bladed Gauntlet bestowed upon him such a speed that he became known as "The Arrow". Of his three brothers, he is the only one sympathetic for his kind. He laments the fall of their great city, and blames himself for their demise. However his loyalty to his brothers' cause outweighs his remorse.

CYCLONE DENOZA
BURNING WHIRLWIND
CHARACTER SHEET

Leather Armbands

Golden Glaives Ignite

KEY DATA

AGE - 36
RACE - Bali Kajaa
WEAPONS - Twinblade
Boomerangs

Twinblade Devastation

Denoza's wish granted him posession of the Twin bladed boomerangs, fierce flaming throwing weapons which ignite anything in their path. His mastery of these blades earned him the nickname "The Cyclone". But few have lived long enough to repeat it. He is merciless and fights only to reveal the true potential of the Dragongate to the world. He resents humanity for ostricizing his kind, and longs only to be feared for his great power. The scars on his armor are tokens, and reminders of his attempts to challenge his older brother.

LOCATIONS
THE WORLD OF TWILIGHT MONK

SPERIA
EASTERN CONTINENT
WORLD MAP

MYSTIC LANDS

To the rest of Speria, the Eastern Continent is known as the "Mystic Lands", due to the stories of supernatural demons and ancient sorcery, sealed demon gates, and many other relics from a forgotten age. Because of that, many bandits and theives travel to these lands in hopes of disappearing forever.

Whereas most of the rest of the world has embraced technology, the Eastern continent rejected much of the automation and mechanization of the new world, and embraced a more spiritual pursuit.

The lush mountains, and open fields preserve the old way of life for many farmers, small time merchants and fisherman. Small cities such as Belgarde exist as a central hub, but it pales in comparison to the meccas found in other continents.

Tokka Hut
- Population - 1.5
- Annual Visitors - 2+
- Faction - Celestial Temple
- Hostility - None

Crescent Isle
- Population - 62 Various locals, 21 Moonkin
- Key Export - Taters
- Annual Visitors - 1200+
- Faction - Neutral

Groblin Ruins
- Population - 28 Groblins
- Annual Visitors - 2+
- Faction - Groblin
- Hostility - High

Sky Temple
- Population – 3
- Annual Visitors – 0
- Faction – Magma Unit
- Hostility – High

NowheresVille
- Population – 13
- Annual Visitors – 0
- Faction – Byronian
- Hostility – Low

Arcturo Village
- Population – 6
- Annual Visitors – 1+
- Faction – None
- Hostility – High

Bandit Cave
- Population – 12
- Annual Visitors – 1+
- Faction – None
- Hostility – High

Tater Town

The town of Crescent Isle sets on an archipelago on the western coast of the largest continent in Speria. It's a fairly under developed location for the most part, but it's location makes it a central hub for many travelers, mostly passing through. Because of this, it's primarily regarded as a trade post. Here you will find many people from all over, buying and selling goods of all kinds. Nothing looks particularly out of place here.

The primary export of Crescent Isle would be "Taters", essentially a sweet potato crop which is farmed on small platforms woven throughout the stone spires that make up the central structure of the island. The locals have also crafted many winding platforms and suspension bridges throughout the town creating many hidden passageways, which only a local may truly know. At the heart of Crescent Isle is the Celestial Temple and Monastery.

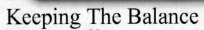

Keeping The Balance

The residents of Crescent Isle are primarily simple farmers and traders, that enjoy the protection of the Moonken at the Celestial Temple, who regard the village as their home and their people, despite their relatively different lifestyles.

The monks of the Celestial Temple can be found in the town square of Crescent Isle with great frequency, and it is possibly the only place in the world where they are quite welcome.

Often, many a traveler will come to Crescent Isle to find rare goods, or to petition the Monks for their help in matters elsewhere in Speria.

Dispite its eclectic culture, foreign cuisine, and rare mix of goods and services, few people decide to stay on the island, and prefer nearby cities such as Belgarde for its more lavish accomodations, casinos, ports, and hotels. These are things which could not be found in Crescent Isle.

Crescent isle is more of the kind of a place for farmers and commoners. The people are friendly, and generous, always helping out their neighbors and visitors.

CRESCENT ISLANDERS
A MIXED MELTING POT
CHARACTER SHEET

Traders and Merchants

Also known as "The Kitchen of Speria", the diversity of food options on the small island are a large draw for travelers on their way to Belgarde.

The residents of Crescent Isle come from all over the world to enjoy the protection of the Monastery, but few remain in any long term capacity. The primary export for the island is their "Taters", but a good number of fishermen psychics, merchants and priests also reside here.

Carpenter

Byakke

Merchant

Priest

Fisherman

Cook

Psychic

Merchant

Western Sanctuary

The Celestial Temple at Crescent Isle is also a Monastery for the Moonken who train there. The temple has stood for several thousand years, and is the last remaining remnant of the Monks of Twilight. Many hidden caverns and sealed off rooms still remain undiscovered within it's walls. Ancient relics and dangerous artifacts are stored within the vaults underneath the central structure, but access to these vaults is extremely Limited. In fact only a few of the masters even know the way through the subteranean maze within the island upon which it's carved.

The temple itself consists of several hundred rooms and was clearly designed to house thousands. However, much of what remains is used for the small number of remaining orphan Moonken quarters, training grounds and libraries.

A Forgotten Village

Just outside of the Frozen Mountain rests a small cluster of cabins. Not many people travel to the Frozen Mountain anymore. But when the Bali Kajaa of the mountain thrived, Arcturo Village served as their conduit to the outside world.

Located at the base of the mountain, only a few small families now reside in the village, including last survivors of the Bali Kajaa. Here they settled with humans to lick their wounds and rebuild their way of life.

However remote it may be, the local blacksmith is a bit of an unknown prodigy. Having lots of freetime over the decades, he has crafted and stockpiled especially powerful blades and armor.

Since the path through was entirely sealed off, Arcturo Village also provides a back entrance to the mountain via a secret cave deep underground known only to a few.

The Cursed Maze

Surrounding the small village of Tuksa is a deadly forest into which all Tuksans fear to venture. The twisting roots and vines of the dead trees penetrate the earth, creating underground passageways and uprooting the soil, displacing the very earth shell upon which the continent is set. This has opened up large, deadly crevaces which are barely visible through the thick layer of mist, leading many travelers to their untimely death. Those who survive and escape the forest often take up refuge in Tuksa, where they chose to live out their remaining years never desiring to face the Dark Forest and its perils again.

It is said that the forest was cursed by a dark magic many hundreds of years ago. But if one were to investigate the abandoned cabin in those woods, he may find evidence of a hermit , packrat wizard, who had cursed the forest with the mere desire to be left to his own devices away from the turmoil and troubles of the world. and mend his wounded heart.

The maze and twisted waterways are home to some of the most vicious creatures imagineable.

Trees twist into hand shapes

Coiled root

Eastern Speria

Tuksa

Oliff's Farm

Valley Of Fear

The village of Tuksa rests in the valley between the Dark Forest the Alippa Mountains. Initially, the village had been constructed as a refuge for travelers who'd gotten lost in the forest, and were fearful to attempt to return through the perilous Dark Forest.

The Village is completely cut off from the outside world. After several generations, the people of Tuksa built barricades to wall themselves in. A sixty foot circular wall was constructed around the village perimiter, where modular homes are stacked on top of each other. These homes can be moved and re-arranged depending on what season catches the best sunlight, or which way the wind pushes the stench from the Dark Forest.

Tuksans were born into fear. Anything that is strange, or could cause any threat to their way of life is thrown outside of their protective fences. This is primarily the reason why they have cast out Olif and his adopted Moonkin child, despite his many contributions to their town.

Within the walls of Tuksa, gondolas and other wired contraptions transport goods leaving little reason for anyone to leave their home or go outside at all. Each night the gates are closed, and streets are lit with torches. The current population is unknown, since much of the village was burned to ashes after the great fire.

A Scoundrels Paradise

Belgarde was originaly an outpost for the Liongate military. In fact, beneath it's stacked structures, and behind the glowing casino signs, rests an armada of rusted old military ships and anti-air emplacements. However, over the past fifty years, it has become over-run by criminal organizations, gangs, two bit thieves, and lawyers. Despite this, there's no better place to acquire rare goods from around the world or make a quick buck.

From across the continent, anyone eager to make their mark on the world, dreams of making it big in Belgarde. However, because local law enforcement is corrupt, crime syndicates control everything from the shipyards to the newspapers.

While the eclectic trading stalls along the docks offer goods from around the world similarly to those found in Crescent isle, most people come to the port city of Belgarde for the lack of law enforcement and deregulation. It's not against any law here to take whatever is unguarded, from goods, to livestock, and even living beings.

Belgarde upholds no laws against theivery, slavery, or piracy.

Gambling contributes the largest source of income to Belgarde, making it the most advanced city in the Eastern continent. Everyone knows the games are rigged, but that doesn't stop them from pouring in from everywhere in the world on the many ships coming in and out of the harbor.

VARIOUS LOCATIONS

The world of Speria is vast and full of places to discover, from sky temples, underground ruins, lava flowing caverns and misty swamps.

BESTIARY
THE WORLD OF TWILIGHT MONK

SLIMES
MINDLESS ENSLAVED SOULS
CHARACTER SHEET

KEY DATA

SIZE - 200-300 lbs
RACE - Formless Soul
WEAPONS - Icicle Throw,
Mouth (Swallow)

Frozen Souls

Ice slimes are a hostile creature born from the vibrating instability of the rift on the fringe of Arcturo Mountain. Once living denizens of the Bali Kajaa, their souls have been ripped from their bodies and converged into the frost so that they may never return to their original form.

Now twisted and soul hungry, they feed on heat energy, and freeze it instantly to sub-zero temparatures, making them grow in size.

Icicles Form From Consumed Heat!

Splitting Spreads The Soul Thin and becomes More Mindless.

Always Losing Mass

The standard ice slime attack is an ice burst which reaches twice it's body width

Ice slimes can go into an ultra "defense mode" that freezes anyone who touches it.

Size comparison with Mao

Larger slimes can eat the player and he must shake loose to break free

NORMAL   FLAT

Slimes can also "go flat" and cannot be attacked in this state.

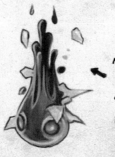

Mostly slimes spawn from cave ceilings or drop from openings on higher ledges

Other Slimes

Ice slimes are only one form of trapped souls. Throughout the world of Speria, there are many variations, including poison slimes, lava slimes, armored and chaos slimes.

GROBLENS
EARTH DIGGERS
CHARACTER SHEET

Repurposed armor

Weapons are all reformed from other parts

KEY DATA

SIZE - 500- 600 lbs
RACE - Groblen
WEAPONS - Assembled
Metal Spikes, Throw Rocks

Outcast Miners

The Groblens on the Eastern continent have never been accepted into most societies, likely due to a complete misunderstanding of language. Their inability to form complete sentences leaves them at a disadvantage when dealing with anyone of any race other than their own. Because of this, they state their emotion after their broken sentences.

Occupying mostly abandoned mines and ruins, they dig deep into the earthshells and trade the treasures they find for scraps of food.

WILDERNESS TROLLS
WARRIOR SPEARBREAKERS
CHARACTER SHEET

SpearBreaker Holes

KEY DATA

SIZE - 160 - 200 lbs
RACE - Troll
WEAPONS - Old Metal
Scrap, Makeshift Spears

Fear The Wild

The Wild Trolls of Speria are a barbaric scavengers. They have no organization or sense of reason. They are simple minded, easily fooled, and will kill for the tiniest of treasures. They pierce their bodies with the armor and weapons they have pillaged. Wild Trolls have strange regenerative abilities allowing them to split bones within their bodies to create spearbreaking holes in their arms.

HOGNOZE NIGHT FLIER
TREASURE BATS
CHARACTER SHEET

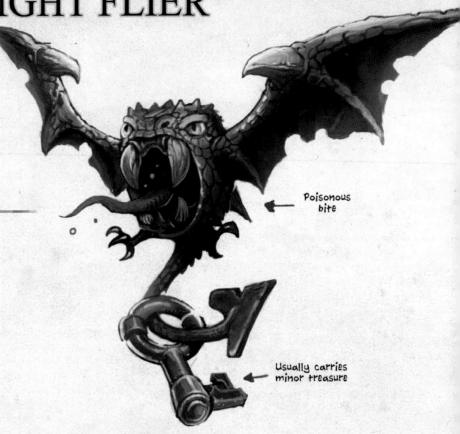

Poisonous bite

Usually carries minor treasure

KEY DATA

SIZE - 10-20 lbs
RACE - Night Flier
WEAPONS - Steal, Poison-
ous bite, Escape

Thief in the Night

Hognoze Bats are nocturnal, and come out at night only to steal treasures. They are known to link together with their vestigal tails to steal weapons and treasures from camping travelers or even from each other. The Hognoze is a selfish creature that hoards its treasure in secret places at higher elevations. If one were to encounter a Hognoze, it generally pays off more to allow it to escape, and follow it back to it's den than to loot the treasure it holds.

AKULA MYST SERPENT
MINIONS OF THE MYST CRYSTAL
CHARACTER SHEET

Crystal infection

Can fire infected quills

KEY DATA

SIZE - 150- 350 lbs
RACE - Serpent
WEAPONS - Infectious
Bite, Tail Whip, Swallow

Fear The Wild

Akula serpents were once garden snakes. However, their bodies have been mutated by a type of Myst crystal.

The crystals constant growth creates a sound which draws the infant serpents to them. Once they embrace the crystal, and begin to feed, their bodies merge, embuing them with the ability to infect others with the same fate.

In time all life forms infected with the disease turn entirely to to crystal, frozen in time for eternity. There is no known cure for this infection.

ONIMEN SUN RIDER
SUN GOD CULTISTS
CHARACTER SHEET

KEY DATA

SIZE - 250 lbs
RACE - Unknown
WEAPONS - Bone Scythe,
Salvaged Scraps and Armor

Clan of The Shattered Sun

Every day, the Onimen Riders decend from the cloud palace of Ono Nalshi and collect living creatures for sacrifice to their sun god "O". They believe that this ritual is the reason for the changing of the night to day, and would die to bring the sun from it's cradle, as they are born from the flowerbed surrounding the Sun palace.

Their leaders chant tales of "the longest night". A day when the sun refused to rise for them. .

ONIMEN MOUNT
DIVINE BEASTS OF ONO NALSHI
CHARACTER SHEET

KEY DATA

SIZE - 800-100 lbs
RACE - Unknown
WEAPONS - Horns, Tail
Gaze

Sun Steed

These Onimen beasts are born in the lower levels of the flowerbed of the Sun Palace, and serve as mounts for the Onimen Riders.. What they lack in intelligence, they more than make up for in strength. They share a mind with their rider since birth, and will stop at nothing to protect them.

Flower petal wings

BARRAKEWDOS
WILD FISH MEN
CHARACTER SHEET

KEY DATA

SIZE - 1-200 lbs
RACE - Barrakewdo
WEAPONS - Harpoons,
Spears, Whipping Tail

Evolution Denied

The warrior Barrakewdos are an evolved race of fish men that have locked themselves away from the rest of civilization beyond the southern mountains of the Eastern continent. It is said that their towers soar to the heavens, and their mines reach as low as the third Earthshell.

The elite aristocrats of their society deny their own evolution by containing themselves in a small fishbowls for generations, leaving those with arms and legs to defend their borders. The smallest of the Barrakewdos is King "Troutmouth", who rules his kingdom from a one gallon glass bowl.

Of course, no one can confirm or deny the validity of any information about the Barrakewdo, since they refuse entry to all outsiders within their city walls.

King Troutmouth

Spear Charge!

Warrior Barrakewdo armor

More Barrakewdo Battle Armor

Admiral Razorven

Commander Carpadium

Prince Tilapior

EPISODES
THE WORLD OF TWILIGHT MONK

THE MAN AND THE MOONKEN
CHILD OF THE MOON
SHORT STORY (2015)

Farmer Olif

Puppy Bartol

Tail of the Tenza

When an infant child falls from the sky, the fearful people of the secluded town of Tuksa see him only as a bad omen. It was as if a Minotaur or otherworldly beast had arrived at their doorstep. But when one farmer steps forward to raise him, both of them are outcast from the rest of the village.

As the child's supernatural abilities began to grow, the villagers continued to blame him for every bad thing that happened, from long winters to missing cats. The tension between them grew, with each passing season, until there was simply no way for the people of Tuksa to share the valley with the lonely farmer and the boy from the sky.

THE MAN AND THE MOONKEN
JOURNEY TO THE WEST
ILLUSTRATED SHORT STORY (2016)

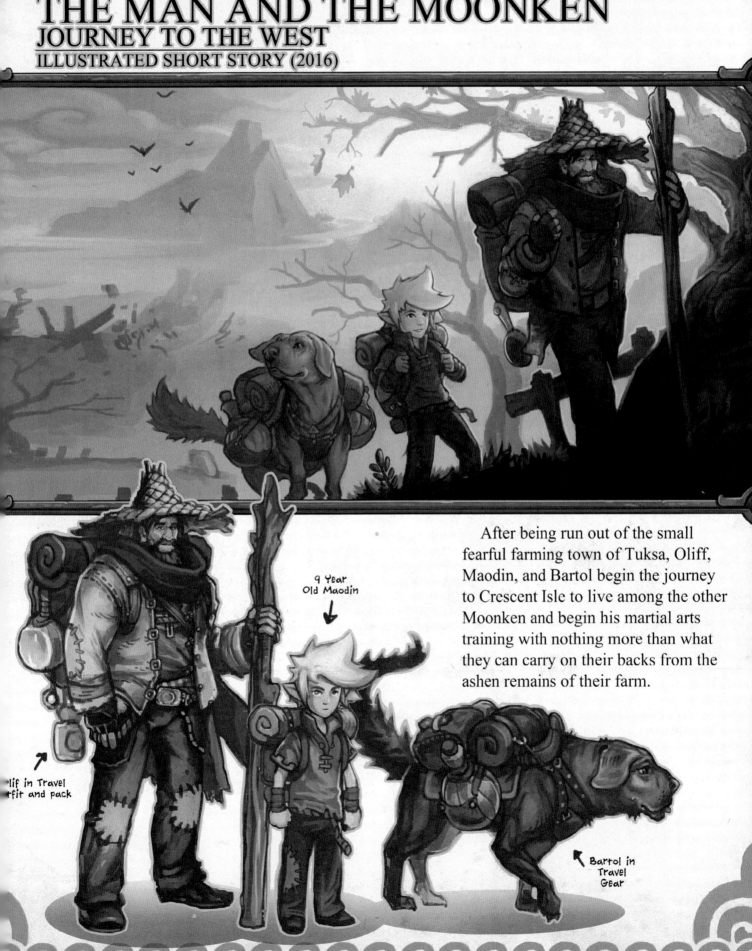

9 Year Old Maodin

...lif in Travel ...fit and pack

Bartol in Travel Gear

After being run out of the small fearful farming town of Tuksa, Oliff, Maodin, and Bartol begin the journey to Crescent Isle to live among the other Moonken and begin his martial arts training with nothing more than what they can carry on their backs from the ashen remains of their farm.

THE BEAST OF TUKSA
LOST IN THE LABYRINTH
ILLUSTRATED SHORT STORY (2018)

Awakening

Their exodus carries them through the perilous and cursed Dark Forest, where they are pursued by a great beast. Hunted and desperate, they hide out in an old upside down Wizards cabin, where Maodin steals a mysterious magical book that eats living things. The book guides them to the exit, which can only be opened once the beast is destroyed.

In the battle with the great beast, Mao is severely wounded, leaving Oliff, his earthfather to wonder if he'd merely led them on a journey to their own demise.

SECRETS OF KUNG FULIO
MONK TRAINEE RAZIEL
ILLUSTRATED NOVELLA (2019)

Looking For Trouble

Having arrived at the Monastery and beginning his training years after the other Moonkin orphans, and taken on a new name, Raziel Tenza had built a reputation for being a very poor student. This made him a prime target for the obnoxious degenerate Nox and his band of cronies, "The Red Cobras".

After suffering a humiliating atomic wedgie, and waking up in a trash bin in a dark alley, Raz's buddy Rin informs him that Nox has challenged him to a public fight in 24 hours.

Having little to no fighting ability, Raz prepares for the worst. Humiliated, pissed off, and smelling just... awful, the duo sets out on a journey to discover the Secrets of something called "Kung Fulio" and get some good old fashioned street justice.

Nox and The Red Cobras

NOX

I gotta lil' extra sumfin for you too.

Backstreet Brawlers

The Red Cobras generally stick to the back alleys of Crescent Isle, and loot unsuspecting or lost travelers. Over the past couple of years, they've built a network of underground tunnels that lead to their lair, giving them quick get-away locations all over the island.

SECRETS OF KUNG FULIO
MONK TRAINEE RAZIEL
ILLUSTRATED NOVEL (2019)

A Fishy Fetch-Quest

Raz and Rin's search for the Secrets of Kung Fulio lead them on a seemingly endless circle of trading this-for-that with local merchants like Jubee, and at times even rescuing them from wandering monsters.

Jubee's Disguise

ILLUSTRATIONS
THE ART OF TWILIGHT MONK

TWILIGHT MONK ™

FROM THE
CREATOR OF
CREED
TRENT KANIUGA

WWW.TWILIGHTMONK.COM

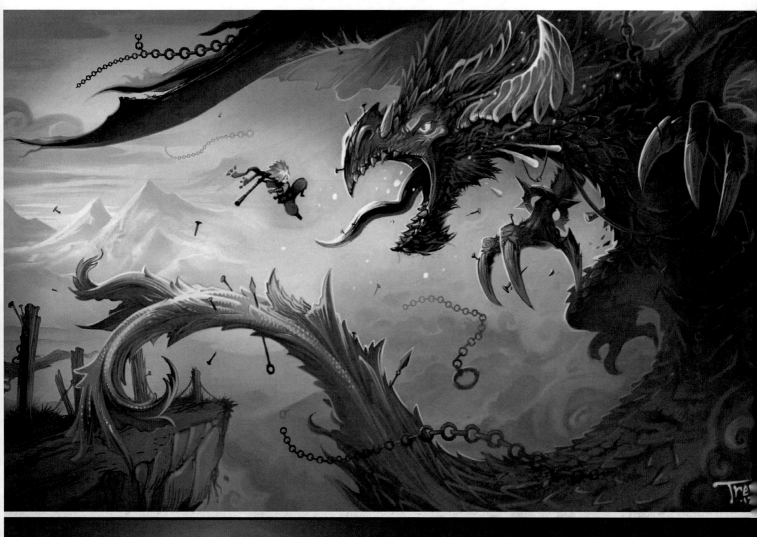

SKETCHBOOK
THE ART OF TWILIGHT MONK

SKETCHBOOK
EARLY DEZMIN EXPLORATION

Dezmin final Hair Design 2007

Dezmin Heads 2006

First Dezmin Sketch 2004

Jacket Redesign 2004

SKETCHBOOK
EARLY RAZIEL/MAODIN DESIGNS 2004

Expressions
2004

SKETCHBOOK
EARLY DESIGNS AND POSES 2002-2003

Early Design 2002

Dezmin battle poses 2003

First sketch design 2002

SKETCHBOOK
EARLY DESIGNS AND POSES 2002-2003

trentkaniuga.com

Early
Design
2002

SKETCHBOOK
EARLY DESIGNS AND POSES 2002-2003

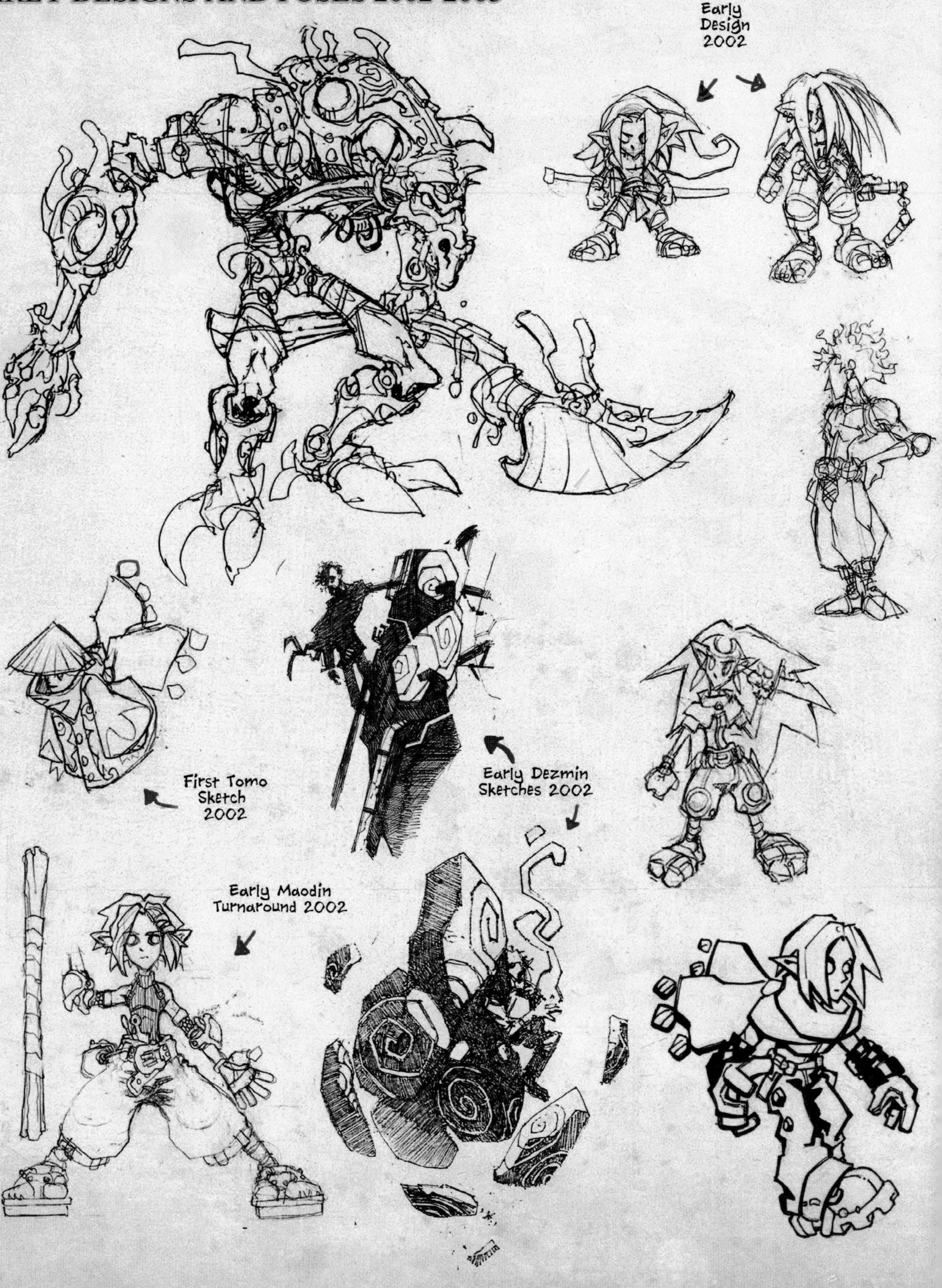

Early
Design
2002

First Tomo
Sketch
2002

Early Dezmin
Sketches 2002

Early Maodin
Turnaround 2002

Dezmin Suit design 2004

Early Gray Design 2002

SKETCHBOOK
EARLY DESIGNS AND POSES 2006-2007

Dezmin Suit design 2006

Dezmin Expressions 2002

SKETCHBOOK
EARLY DESIGNS AND POSES 2006-2007

Alt Monastery robes design
2007

Expressions
2007

SKETCHBOOK
UNUSED DESIGNS

SKETCHBOOK
EARLY CRESCENT ISLE 2002-2003

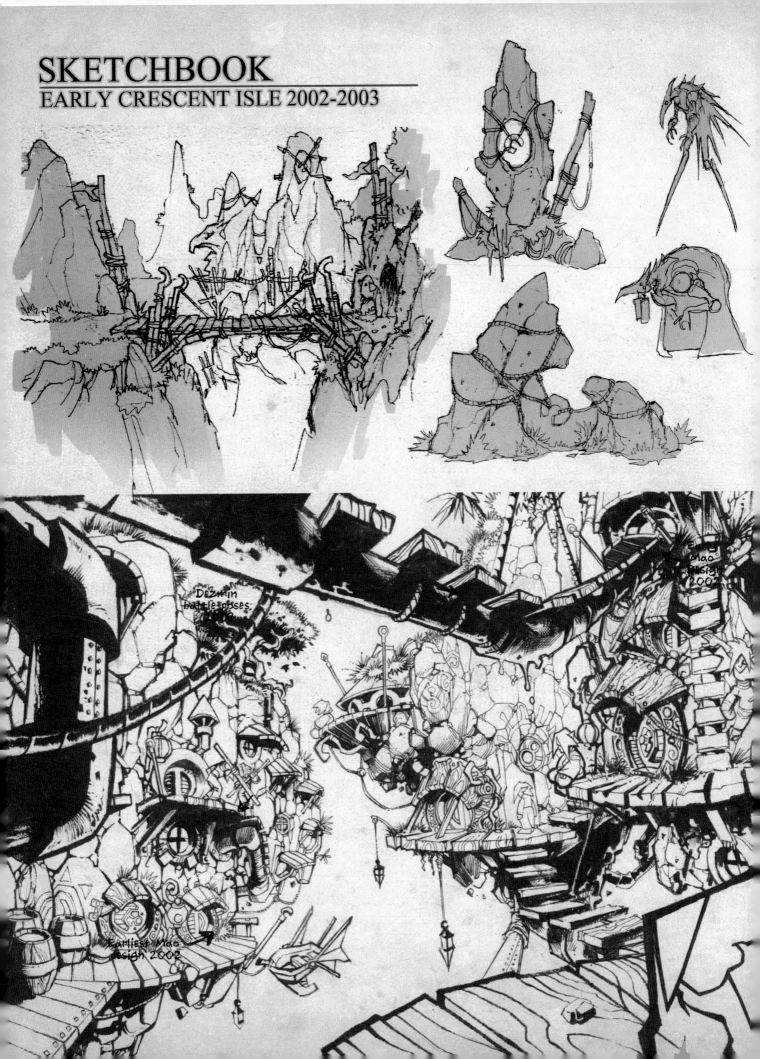

Dezmin
battle poses

Early
Mao
design
2002

Earliest Mao
design 2002

Made in the USA
Las Vegas, NV
25 November 2024